AN ENDLESS HUNGER

NARCISSE NAVARRE

AN ENDLESS HUNGER

Edited by Marzio Ombra & RJ Locksley

Cover model: Andrei Andrei

Published by Digital Alchemist, LLC

ISBN: 978-0-9846654-2-6

Printed in the United States of America.

ACKNOWLEDGEMENTS

I began writing *An Endless Hunger* in the summer of 1998 and worked on it slowly for nearly ten years. It could be said that this story is what started it all.

I owe a debt of gratitude to all the people who have encouraged and supported my writing: To my dear friend Marzio Ombra for working tirelessly by my side on our writing projects. To my editor, RJ Locksley, whose nipping and tucking has made this book shine. To talented Andrei Andrei for believing in me and lending his sexiness to the book trailer and cover. To my husband for scoring the trailer and going along with my crazy idea of becoming a writer. And last, but not least, the readers who have taken a chance on me.

Thank you.

Dedicated to my father,
the man who taught me to dream.

HER LIPS WERE RED, HER LOOKS WERE FREE,
HER LOCKS WERE YELLOW AS GOLD:
HER SKIN WAS AS WHITE AS LEPROSY,
THE NIGHTMARE LIFE-IN-DEATH WAS SHE,
WHO THICKS MAN'S BLOOD WITH COLD.

THE RIME OF THE ANCIENT MARINER
—SAMUEL TAYLOR COLERIDGE

Through the years, all those nameless, bloodless bodies had been swallowed by the night, their beautiful features contorted in a final grimace of pain and regret. Some struggled before their death, spewing threats and curses. Others prayed silently as their minds searched for closure to an otherwise unexciting existence. Some found relief in death. They were my least favorite.

The very pretty ones I kept for a while, until their nagging grew tiresome. I kept them caged up, beneath the floor. When I was most *ennuyé*, I played with them. Like everything else, however, my games soon bored me. In fact, the entire process was becoming quite tedious.

IT WAS FRIDAY, NOVEMBER SOMETHING. I COULD NOT REMEMBER.

The sky groaned under the weight of the storm. Heavy rain was falling. Beneath jagged arcs of lightning, flickering streetlights threatened to withdraw their meager illumination. Each individual bead of water sparkled like a well-cut diamond before meeting the filthy pavement. I floated in that sea of scintillating light until the world was like an old Noir film, black and white. Droplets made their way down my face as I stood silently, an eternal being without direction or purpose. Alone.

1

I felt the hunger stir within my hollowness. I felt the need, stronger than sex, rise inside me—red hot and burning. I could feel in my ancient bones the desire to return to ash, to crumble into dust. I was a walking collection of memories and cruelty, nothing more than a wreck of my former self. The idealistic child who once carried my birth name was destroyed long ago. With each death—each exquisite, gurgled scream—his hope for Man had vanished.

From the corner of my eye I saw what I had been waiting for. The cab screeched to a stop. Slamming the car door, the girl alighted. Her tangled, shoulder-length hair was plastered against her pale skin. She wore a long coat that briskly soaked up the gutter water as she stepped into a deep puddle. Cursing, she attempted to make herself presentable but gave up quickly, wagering I wouldn't care when the clothes came off.

I could smell the trepidation along her skin, bubbling just beneath the surface. In spite of the cold, sweat beaded between her breasts. Her hands trembled as she switched the black duffel bag from one hand to the other.

She looked in my direction. "Hello?"

The distinct click of her heels thrilled me as she walked in my direction. Anna's voice was like the sound of very fine crystal when you toasted somebody's good health. Perfect.

"Are you Michael?" she asked, voice cracking.

I nodded.

"Then I'm your girl," she said, wiping the rain from her eyes.

My silence made her doubt.

"Are you just going to stand there?"

The fact that she didn't run was proof that she did not see a monster. What did she see? I wondered.

2

"Look, maybe this is a bad idea," she said as I emerged from the halo of the streetlight.

—No. Please don't go.

I approached her petite form. She shuddered. She had large, brown eyes bordering on hazel. Her mouth was small, shaped like a fine recurve bow. I fought the hunger back as it gnawed my insides. It would have to wait. Putting my arm around her small shoulders, we walked away, into the night.

"By the way, my name is Anna. The agency told me you had requested me because of it. I thought it was a bit odd but odd's not bad, you know? I don't mind."

She paused as we crossed the avenue, then continued, "So, do you like... have a thing for Annas? Not that it's that strange, I mean some guys have a thing for chicks in pantyhose or—"

I looked down at her and smiled.

"I guess I'm a bit nervous, that's all."

She was embarrassed about carrying on. Anxiety exuded from her body like sweet perfume. I desired her and in that moment I was Man again. I was flawed by my urgent need for Woman—for Her.

—There is something musical about the name. In ancient Hebrew it is pronounced Hannah. It means grace.

"Really?"

She wasn't interested. I was probably bunched in her mind with the foot fetishists.

—Anna is a beautiful name for a beautiful woman.

"Where are we going, anyway?"

—Central Park West.

This new girl reminded me of the ancient Madonnas of Renaissance art. She wasn't thin or frail, she was real, like my Anna long ago. Her soaked garments swayed with each step, molding to the voluptuous curves of her body. I took in every bit of her, drinking my fill of her wild, disheveled beauty. I followed the raindrops as they rolled down her forehead, then curved over her cheeks like sterling tears. With each step, I felt my heart stir. Beauty always had a profound effect.

Rain tapered to a trickle before ceasing entirely. Wet, black streets reflected our shadows as we crossed time and time again. Our journey was mostly a quiet one. Anna was uncomfortable in my presence and didn't bother to hide it. I sensed her detachment. Like all the others, she wanted the night to be over before it began.

Beneath the weight of my arm, Anna bobbed along, unable to match my long strides. Heels were not exactly conducive to getting anywhere fast. I didn't care. Time was irrelevant.

We were drenched to the bone as we left the sanctuary of the streetlights behind. Darkness engulfed us as we entered the park. Beside me, Anna came to a halt, pulling her arm free of my grasp.

"Look, I've had enough of this shit. Where the fuck are you taking me?"

The scent of consternation turned to bitter fear.

—It's just a shortcut, come with me.

My suggestion resonated inside her like a plucked string. Her heartbeat slowed and her pupils dilated. I extended my hand.

—Please?

Where the tips of Anna's fingers met mine, a gentle pulse spread. The scent of musky arousal mingled with her fear in a delightful cocktail. I inhaled, comfortable knowing she was mine.

Skeletal trees swayed to a macabre dance as our footsteps sank into the muddy ground. Anna followed without complaint, mesmerized by the power of my plea. We descended the massive stone stairs that led to the fountain of the angel—my angel. In the darkness, copper-green wings were black against the moonless sky.

I led my beautiful captive behind the stairs, where an overgrown patch of vines and thorns opened to reveal a hole.

We moved silently along the network of desolate tunnels beneath the park. We zigzagged through the inky blackness until we reached the rusted metal door that held the secret of my oblivion.

Pushing it wide open, I smiled.

—After you, Mademoiselle.

The air was stale with the smell of urine and blood. As we emerged into the salon I saw Anna's face light up at the sight of gleaming gold. I wasn't a lover of velvet or of gold, but there was a particular quality in some materials that appealed to my sense of illusory warmth. I could not perceive warmth in typical ways so I collected things that made me feel hot inside when I gazed upon them—like women.

Women! Glorious women! They lined my halls in their golden splendor. Some reached out, others wept. Some were frozen mid-scream. Like Michelangelo's Prigioni, my girls were forever trapped in their casted-metal prisons. Golden women with golden seams, my lovers and victims—contorted, crooked, elevated—gleaming!

Juliet's sublime image rose above the rest. Her golden arms were folded to her chest as she held herself in solitary pain. I adored the way her skin folded slightly at the waist and the curve of her perfect belly. I had lovingly carved for her a marble pedestal, blue-veined and cold. I placed her in the center of two extravagantly long blue velvet strips that hung heavy from their ceiling hooks. Nights ago, when my mood was dark and handsome, I dreamed about her. Since then, she had become my favorite. I had worshipped at her feet, losing myself in her gleaming curves. I left only to feed, and even that lost its luster compared to my golden Queen.

—Beautiful, gentle Juliet. Mine. Forever...

I saw her for the first time in the house of Capulet, when I was young and fair. Juliet sat with her back to the window reading Shakespeare in the midst of all that Jazz. Her downcast eyes were naive, not pure. She was like a porcelain idol, one that you might find cloaked in sequins in a poor man's church. Her hair was done like Ingrid Bergman's. I imagined what it would be like to comb her long, dark hair. It seemed as if she had never let it down. The backs of her legs were painted with a flawless black line. Nylons were scarce and she was prudish.

When Juliet sighed my fragile world almost collapsed. The way she arranged her collar was a signal of love. I accepted. Blue flashed before my eyes as blood-red lips brushed against mine. Heavy perfume. Juliet, you are, were, will be perfect beauty through a glass of brandy wine. Juliet, I never knew your name...

"Are you an artist?" Anna asked, her eyes fixed upon the golden statue.

Voices from the past, the opera and the incessant sound of ocean crashed into me. Suddenly I was aware of everything—everything that I could neither comprehend nor escape. The sounds of the mice and roaches scurrying about were monstrous. The phantom noises were a maelstrom of a nightmare that folded inwards to oppress me. I knew God's intention was to drive me mad, but I refused to let Him do this to me. He would not win, because I would not let him.

Warmth escaped from my outstretched hands. It bled out of me in the form of a single tear. Behind Anna, I caught a glimpse of my contorted features in an age-spotted mirror, Christ-like, crying blood. I wiped my face, as if to erase what was there, then turned away.

Art? Art! I abhorred the word! I was a cursed wretch filled with hatred. I was haunted by misery, followed by calamity, punished by God! I dreamed, and in dreaming woke to find myself suffering. All I had was my capacity to destroy, to hurt, to steal, to lie to myself and others, to formulate banal illusions of creativity. I could not sculpt, I casted. I could not compose, I copied. Although I did not deny the existence of a soul, I knew that mine was damned. Incapable of inspiration, I was nothing but a thief who stole from life to add to Death's collection. I was his tool, his pawn, and his servant. I was the clown who never smiled. I was an empty vessel, void of life. Art from pain was a necessity, not the work of genius. What was genius if not the work of the Divine, that righteous force that opposed my very existence? I was not an artist. I could never be!

En ese momento quise gritar!

An inner scream imploded between my ribs. I felt as if I were about to be wrenched apart. I heard the golden women's laughter. I heard their gossipy whispers. Golden stares burned my flesh. My head ached, if that was possible, and I felt an unquenchable anger overcome me before I found my voice.

—An artist? No, not quite.

I laughed.

My divine gift was my affinity for cowardliness. Like Magdalenes and Marys, the golden women were my *mea culpa*, the albatrosses slung around my neck, the heavy chains I had built in life—or was it death? I felt small and dirty like the mice that made my cave their home. The chandelier's dim light took on a milky, garish-yellow, fish-belly-white hue. I felt wholeheartedly disgusted.

Again.

"It was just a question. I didn't really mean anything by it."

Silence.

Anna smiled. "Beautiful piano, do you play?" Her fingers caressed the dusty edge of the painted clavichord. "If you like, I could play something."

—You play the piano?

"Yes, a little."

—Play something then.

Anna took her coat off and let it drop to the floor. I sat in my customary seat facing love-stricken Juliet. Rusted hinges creaked as she raised the clavichord's fall to reveal ancient, cracked keys. Dust flew into the air.

Even before a single note rang out I was already bored.

Anna's fingers caressed the bone keys, gauging their weight. The instrument was daintier than she was used to. Awkward notes lingered in the cavernous heights before striking my ears like thunder. Anna's trembling hands were piteous conduits for Scarlatti's fabled instrument. The scene was blasphemous, the music jarring, yet I continued to listen. I stared into the emptiness, lost in the disharmony of it all.

When the music stopped, I heard the rustling of paper as Anna leafed through my moldy librettos. I felt a sudden urge to rip them from her, but resisted. What would it matter if she played my music–Death's music? Like the rest of my cave, my compositions were seemingly warm, but cold beneath, like winter.

I looked at my hands. They hadn't changed. They were worn and callused from the hard years at sea, yet they continued to be the hands of a young man. Beneath the floor the others struggled against their restraints. Perhaps the sound of music renewed their hope of freedom. Their enthusiasm struck a chord.

Stirred by their rebelliousness, I slipped unnoticed behind the curtains. Anna's hammer-struck prelude chased me down the stone stairs. The smell of my prisoners' sweaty, unwashed flesh stung my nostrils, but not my sensibilities. I rather enjoyed the stench of human horror.

The women beneath the stairs squirmed against their bonds, hoping that by some miraculous chance, the ropes would come undone. They could not imagine that they would die in a putrid hole, famished, or worse–eaten. No, each of them, and their pathetic little ego, dreamed they would escape to see the light of day. They were wrong.

As I approached, they quieted, praying I would ignore them. Each wished death upon the other. There was no sense of union among these poor souls. It wasn't civilized at all.

Maddeningly attracted by the smell of menstrual blood, I directed my attention to the skinny Asian girl in the corner. Desperately, the girl tried to clench her legs together. Did she think I would not notice the rich, dark blood that pooled between her thighs?

She tried to scream, but I was already upon her. I tugged the pulleys hard, wrenching her off the floor like a marionette. The rope tightened around her thighs, waist, breasts, and neck until she gasped for air. With another tug I spread her legs open until she was levitated entirely–an exquisite butterfly. Her skin became purple as the ropes corralled her circulation.

Crawling beneath her, I began to lick her flow. There was something sacrilegious in the act that made me feel excruciatingly hot. I suckled her juices, lapping at her like a dog, then bit the back of her knee for a fresh mouthful. Tearing into ligament and muscle, I drank. Delicious!

She let out a frantic whimper, then fainted. Lack of oxygen was a mercy. When I let her down, her breathing picked up, but her reprieve was temporary.

My prisoners could expect to live as long as a dozen fresh-cut roses. After a few days their cheekbones wilted against the bones of their once-pretty faces, followed by their bodies. It never ceased to amaze me how quickly beauty rotted and decomposed. It saddened me to see my playthings go.

Tossed away like rags, their deaths added to my torment. During the hours of garish sun, their desiccated memories lay with me–such was the fate of the damned.

Rising from the floor, I looked for my next snack. There were nearly ten of them now.

"Mister, please," one of them called out, "please, for the love of God, let me go. I promise I won't tell anyone. Not a soul."

It was the typical request, coming from the typical girl I had kidnapped a week ago. I walked over to her and petted her matted hair. She cringed. I lifted her bound wrist and bit deep, almost to the bone. As I drank to the music of her screams, she convulsed. Slowly her eyes rolled upward in search of a savior that would never come. I counted heartbeats as they galloped, then trotted, then crawled... to a stop. Nine hundred and thirty six beats transpired before she slumped listlessly–forever silenced.

The others' eyes would have jumped from their sockets were it not for their lids. They screamed and writhed, flies caught in my webs. I released the girl's bleeding wrist and crawled away from her. I had gorged beyond comfort. Against the raucous cacophony, I bent over, allowing the coagulated globs to drip from my mouth.

The remaining blood raced through my starving cells. My head swam in the opiate sensation. As I closed my eyes, bright colors, unimaginable by the human mind, danced before me, twisting and stretching with the woeful notes of the clavichord. The notes themselves seemed to recede into an eternity only to jump back into my ears with the force of the ocean. Waves of heat washed over me and I experienced, as always, that carefree floating feeling that came exclusively after having killed.

I lay unmoving. Quiet. To anyone other than my kind I would have seemed dead–I mean truly dead. When the colors subsided and the notes became tolerable I began to think again. I tried to picture Anna's naked splendor, but her image was replaced by Juliet and then... by God.

Countless years had not taught me restraint. I looked down at myself. I was covered in blood. I felt like a mindless buffoon. There had been no need to feed a second time, much less to be sloppy. I undid the bonds that held the dead girl's body and slung her over one shoulder. Soon her bones would join the pile.

I sat the dead girl at the edge of a plastic barrel and pushed down. The container was barely large enough to fit a body. My least favorite part was having to break their legs, but I tended to side with practicality. A loud crack rang out followed by another. The girl's knees bent back and she slid all the way down. Only her toes peeked from the edge and soon they too would disappear.

The acid worked wonders. Within minutes the violent chemical reaction began to disintegrate flesh. The runaway floated in a sea of her own fleshy flotsam, bobbing in the bubbling acid bath. It was despicable.

Choking on the fumes of their dead comrade, my prisoners begged to be released. They shrieked and begged and cried and carried on as if I had even a shred of humanity to spare—pathetic, really. Within a day the girl in the barrel would be consumed. I would neutralize the acid with magnesium-lime and the messy pulp of her shell would seep through the corroded grate all the way to the river. The typical girl would depart this world down a drain. No one would miss a drugged-up, homeless junkie who had begged for spare change.

Even deep beneath the ground, I could feel the dawn rise inside my bones. Morning always brought a lazy feeling that spread from the tip of my limbs, working itself inwards until it reached my rotten core. I had fought dawn's magic before, but the curse always won.

I closed the impregnable door behind me and scurried up like a wounded animal. For the first time since I had returned to my hole with Anna in tow, the emptiness became almost violent. The thunder of the notes had ceased. Anna had stopped playing. I zigzagged past her sleeping form, moving as fast as the wind that once carried me to distant shores. I slipped past my golden women and sprang along the industrial staircase that led to the semi-final floor of my abode.

The second floor smelled of moisture and moss. The walls were wet and still wept from the day's downpour. The lavish wooden furniture had begun to rot. Magnificent chandeliers, having lost their grandeur, hung like rusted ribs. Long ago I had taken up the habit of hanging tapestries along the walls to absorb the decay and moisture. I had collected only the finest pieces.

My most faithful wall rug still hung in relatively good condition above the dilapidated stairs. It was embroidered brightly in aquas, oranges and golds and it told the story of the Anna Kristina, that fabled ship that sailed into the Spanish sunset, ne'er to return to shore. The Anna Kristina had been frozen in time by the exquisite threads as she rocked in the dark, storm-tossed sea. If I concentrated, I could almost hear the sound of the ocean and the song of the Lorelei as they seduced the massive spice ship deeper and deeper into the whirlwind. Sirens sang with outstretched arms, flooding men's minds with Lust and Oblivion. Golden threads woven into golden women whose skin shone like the sun illuminated the Anna Kristina's final destiny.

—How many times had I moored in thee, Anna?

The memory of Anna's taste and smell and wildness seared my insides. These distant memories always came at the last minute, before daybreak, only to disperse and become unattainable as the day's nightmares replaced her mischievous smile. I looked forward to the time right before sunrise, when I looked up into nothingness. I yearned to find myself marooned in some imaginary place where everything was possible and I could lie motionless in the expanse of Anna's loving arms. My breathing came in short gasps as that glorious orb rose above the trees and the buildings, illuminating the waking world–a world that, for countless years, I had only seen in the blue of night. I thought of her, my Anna, before sinking into the moist patch of earth that accepted me. Indigo shadows danced beyond the promenades. As my lids closed, the twisted world faded. My mind, filled with a thousand screams and lamentations, knew no sleep.

I was a sailor, *marinero*, just off the spice ships that docked along the island coast. I had left my country the day of my mother's death. She was buried in a borrowed dress, her stiff fingers clutching a wooden rosary. I should have killed him, the priest, God's servant who raped her, but I was a coward. Long months of watered rum, picked fish and the stench of salt tied her memory into a knot at the pit of my belly. The sea and those leathery, cracked faces had hardened my will. I had become a man, or so I thought.

When my wobbly sea legs stepped into the *taverna*, I was seduced by the whirlwind of a worn red skirt and sparkling laughter. Anna! She ignited life in every pair of rum-reddened, sleepless eyes. Soft and luxuriant, her body carried with it the knowledge of Man's short and most vulnerable eternity.

She was a whore in the most beautiful sense of the word. Anna's every move provoked desire. She loved all and accepted all, carried them from that bug-infested bed to a place where their spirit could climb, soar and finally rest upon her loving breast. She was the sun itself, and I the moth seeking to end my days in her radiance.

I recalled vividly the first time my hands wrapped around her slender waist. I inhaled her spicy island skin like a starved man, quaffing deep until the ocean was a distant memory. Along the length of her glorious curves I found my home and in her pleasured cries–my death. As surely as a sailor lured by the fabled sirens, I drowned in Anna's liquid grave of love.

I lay awake soaked in my own blood—others' blood—as my eyes cried their secret guilt and my hands clawed the earth in anger. I drowned beneath the earth each day, suffocating without choice, with the knowledge that I would awaken yet again to repeat the routine of hundreds of nights past. I could not rest. I would not die. I could not stop my mind from thinking, or my soul from burning. Eternity was my punishment, and every night I cursed God out loud. No one heard.

Sometimes I thought I heard the Earth, or things stirring in the earth. It terrified me. My body became excruciatingly frigid as I returned to death. I was a bloated corpse–rotting. I questioned! I questioned everything, and had no answers. I had tried to rationalize my existence. I had gone to great lengths to educate myself, to seek comfort in philosophy, in poetry, in cynicism, but I had found nothing that could provide me with even a minute's peace.

Yes, I spoke Latin and Hebrew and at least a dozen other languages. I could quote a thousand visionaries of our time. I was able to recite, without error, the Canterbury Tales and the Iliad. I played Beethoven, Vivaldi, Chopin and Smetana as if it were my own music. I had attempted to paint like the great Impressionists and Romantics. I collected and studied original works by Rodin, Edison, Braque, Rousseau, Bosch, Pirandello, and many others including Goya, Dali and Confucius.

I had met many of these prolific people. I had laughed and pretended to share wine with them. I listened closely, hanging on each and every word that came from their prolific mouths, hoping for that miracle called inspiration, that divine something which forms at the pit of your stomach, and then rises into your chest with such great feeling that you can hardly breathe. I tried to embrace, from the very beginning, the flair of the times. I socialized with both the rich and the poor and they taught me nothing. These interactions only served to augment the repugnance I felt towards Man.

I lived through times of peace, of war, of sickness, and death. I saw. I heard. I learned nothing! Nothing that could quench my pain. Nothing that could reverse my spiritual decay. Nothing was, is, will be all there is. I had seen women who looked like animals and known animal women. I had heard men speak who you would swear sounded like horses. I had met dog people who barked at others and butterfly children who soared above the noise. Then there were the larvae, those that ate each other until there were no more flies. Occasionally, I experienced earthly brilliance. I passionately envied those who blinded me and made my eyes bleed like fountains. In those rare moments I recoiled back into my grotto sick with envy, yet burning inside, as if stung by a million morning suns.

I was wretched, and in my wretchedness I was needy. All my earthly possessions, as if they mattered, were stockpiled in my subterranean hole. Beauty both eased and intensified my pain and I needed it so that I could feel something, or imagine that I could. I preferred some dismal scrap of feeling, whether grief or warmth or envy, over nothing. Nothing, being the furthest thing from everything, meant madness—something that I had vowed never to succumb to.

The few mementos that had belonged to the loves of my life no longer existed. I imagined these tokens buried at the bottom of the ocean somewhere, undisturbed in their watery graves. It was a lie, of course, but it fit my sense of the dramatic. It was very possible that I had crushed the things dear to me in a senseless fit of rage.

The day went by sluggishly, and my dreams dragged out maliciously, like weeds. I dreamed of the city, of Anna, and the homeless girl bubbling in the acid bath. I saw the nimble fingers gliding along the clavichord. Juliet walked off her pedestal in a flash of shocking blue. As my golden women condemned me, I remembered Shakespeare. *One fire burns out another's burning; One pain is lessen'd by another's anguish.*

In the midst of my dream, I awoke, screaming.

At sunset my body dematerialized against my will. I experienced a buoyant sensation, then felt the essence of my body rise. I wasn't sure what I looked like rising up from beneath the earth or how the wraith-like process took place. At the surface, I coalesced, becoming a most loathsome thing—Man. It was an involuntary occurrence that I had not learned to control.

The chill stabbed me like needles. I walked over to a sawed-off, rusty pipe that doubled as my bathroom and cast my bloody clothes aside. I would burn them later. Sticking my head beneath the icy stream, I scrubbed the blood out of my hair. I bathed before dressing in the habitual uniform of modern man—blue jeans and a T-shirt.

My sharp, predatory senses, propelled by hunger, picked up Anna's sweet scent. The thought of her honeyed blood made my mouth water with anticipation. I imagined that I would attempt to make love to her. I closed my eyes and let the shadows transform into her image. I longed to lay my young-old hands on her smooth skin. I wanted to feel the beating of her heart until she wilted, like the rest of my roses. I desired to feel like a man.

I descended from my hollowed-out sanctuary. Midway down I let out a high-pitched howl that echoed twenty-fold. My body felt warm with thoughts and I wondered how the evening would play itself out. No doubt Anna had brought some fanciful outfit in that black duffel bag of hers. I hoped it would be blue. Suddenly, I felt playful, almost happy.

On my way down I patted the tapestry and watched out of the corner of my eye as the mermaids' undulating movement sent thick puffs of dust and dirt into the air. I willed my withered lungs to inhale that air—my air—and that was when the realization dawned on me. I stopped, then listened and listened once again. I knew instinctively that there was no life, no breath, not a single thing living left in my hole. The only thing that remained of her was the sweetness of her perfume. The scent lingered in the staleness, a foreign element, reminding me of her absence. I opened my mind to her, but only an echo returned. Anna was no longer under that spell which would have forced her to remain. She was gone.

—Anna!

I looked towards the clavichord. Anna's gray knitted scarf was there, untouched. Dust had settled on the spot where the girl had sat. My music sheets were neatly stacked where I had left them. Anna had surely been a figment of my imagination, a dream—a ghostly apparition. The golden women faced away from me, and on this night Juliet seemed old and fragile, like a brittle leaf.

At first the realization brought angst to the pit of my stomach. I sat down on the bottom step and rested my elbows on my knees. I looked up and down and sideways and pretended to stretch my neck. The more I thought about it, the more the whole ordeal was ridiculous. I, the archfiend, had been tricked by a pack of half-witted little girls, whom I assumed had confessed all their dirty little secrets to the police. I tried to imagine them following their ghostly Joan of Arc up to the surface towards the light of day. Did my quiet angel see them leave?

I laughed.

The thought of police complication cramped my style. I began thinking of a possible new identity. I disliked the police as much as I disliked all organized groups. The police were no better than the rats that made my cave their home. The city was crawling with them. Through sheer numbers alone, they would find me.

It was only a matter of time before one of their kind would develop an obsession with the mystery and would pursue me night and day. His commitment to "justice" would make him a hero, and at night he would dream about the medal and the brief TV coverage that would come from capturing someone like me. Mister Astute Cop, whoever he was, would eventually pass the information to the FBI, and those dogs would know exactly where to look. All they had to do was follow the acid trace upwind.

I shifted uncomfortably as something gnawed the back of my mind. I looked out into the vastness of my cave, at the statues, at Juliet. The melancholy set in. All that I was occupied the room before me. Age. That was what I saw, age, and in that rot I thrived, hidden from society like a madman.

Lining the walls were dusty Baroque mirrors to reflect the meager light that seeped in from an as-of-yet undiscovered aperture. Old reflected old, mocking all that was once beautiful, and now, beautifully stale. Gazing into those mirrors reflected a perfect lie. I remained beautiful, young—a poster boy posing for a fragrance campaign? What a joke!

Some mirrors had broken long ago. I had never bothered to pick up the pieces. The sea-blue color of the velvet curtains was dulled by dust. For the first time I noticed that the strips of cloth were ripped and tattered.

—Let the shards fall where they may.

The hole was quiet now. The absence of trapped moans made me nervous. Although my ears welcomed the silence, I was bored by the prospect of an empty basement. I prized my prisoners' suffering–their utter lack of freedom and strength. Already I missed the rush of toying with them, of driving them crazy and watching in horror as they frothed away into nothingness. My prisoners were gone, and with them my sick, demented routine.

Replacing the old with the new, what a concept! Modern times seemed to be ruled by this philosophy of wastefulness. I had seen husbands, married for twenty years, swap their old ladies for eighteen-year olds. Perfectly useful chrome toasters were tossed out to make way for new trendy plastic ones.

Television! There was the method to their madness. This age loved the flickering box that would tell them to throw out the old every winter and buy the new every spring. The new became the old in a matter of weeks.

Plastic surgeons were among the nobility of the age. There were many like myself, beautifully stale. They emerged from the surgeons' clinics with new faces, new hair, thinner, but I knew the truth. They were living mummies. Their insides never reflected their outsides. Their organs rotted and their health failed–slowly, but surely. Natural beauty was rare, temporary and intense, like butterflies. The city had its handful of butterflies, especially in the wintertime when everything froze and the frigid air stung like millions of knives.

I felt lazy. Disconcerted. Lacking. My body slowed to a lethargic hum. Outside the air was thin with frost. The streets were a haphazard pattern of headlights that threatened to intersect at any minute if not for the stop and go of the streetlights. First green then red and yellow until—it seemed—all the cars merged leaving bright trails in the twilight. Yellow cabs and buses carried tired-faced passengers who leaned, defeated, against the foggy windows. I saw two lovers duck and disappear beneath the sidewalk and into the subway holding hands. The stark, urban monotony was broken by the flashing, multicolored lights of Christmas. They pulsed in sequence, first a happy green, then white, blue, red and so on. Some of these displays played Christmas tunes. The electronic buzz of one of the songs assaulted me as I passed a liquor store.

He sees you when you're sleeping,
He knows when you're awake,
He knows if you've been Bad or Good...
—So be good for goodness' sake!

Just yesterday it was mid-November. The thought of it being December, almost Christmas, was mind-boggling. Time, they said, was a fourth dimension. I could not understand its effects on me any better than I could understand what I was. I had stopped trying to understand time, to control it and to know it. Time did not matter. So what if there was an entire month missing from my memory? It didn't bother me in the least. Had Time been this cruel to me while I was growing up? Probably, most likely. In fact I wondered why humans feared Death as opposed to Time. It was Father Time who was the culprit in our demise—their demise!

Outside of the liquor store, an old Arab beggar paced slowly in my direction, jiggling his dirty tin can. He was shivering, drawing his rags about him in an effort to fight the cold—a disease that attacked him from all sides. Times had changed and change was no longer enough of a charity. The old man was a survivor, but I knew that if I gave him too much he would walk directly into the liquor store and drink himself to death. His rheumy stare made me feel young, like a child, as if he could see right through me and kick my conscience in the ass. I didn't like that... having a conscience.

Drone feet carried men and women somewhere where they would most probably shower, eat and sleep. Most would wake up the next morning to wash, rinse and repeat. It was all quite simple actually, not very different from what I myself did every night. My feet carried me to and from my hole where I would eat and sleep and leave once again in search of Anna. Where could she be–the one who made me this way?

I walked west, across town and into the subway. My fare came in a plastic card these days with a magnetic strip along one end. Rechargeable. I shrugged. The roaring wind within the tunnel announced the arrival of the E. After the ding-dong of the doors, I slipped in with a dozen weary passengers. I leaned on a pole as the train lurched forward. The fluorescents gave everyone a sickly color and their faces under that light looked even more disturbed, more tired and dead, as if the people of this city were merely hosts, their bodies vessels for something else altogether more sinister. Perhaps that was how I looked, tired and dead. Did they notice anything different at all?

I never understood why the subway trains had large, Plexiglas windows. It wasn't like anyone could see anything but darkness beyond. There was barely a foot of space on either side of the tunnel. Surely the windows were an aesthetic addition, but why? Did the windows afford some imaginary mental comfort? Did people feel safer thinking that they could potentially jump out in case of an emergency? I saw passengers looking out into the darkness all the time, as if passing before them was a beautiful countryside with tall cypress trees and sweet-smelling flowers. Was the frightening aspect of being closed in having to look inward and connect with each other? The windows provided an excuse to look away and avoid each other—even if looking away resulted in a blasted, black tunnel with unending wires. I focused. I tried to look out into the darkness as intensely as some of my fellow passengers. Whatever comfort they found beyond the tunnel eluded me.

A woman in her mid-twenties wearing the corporate uniform of suit and heels looked up from beneath her thick lashes. Exquisite dark eyes were nearly obscured by overwrought mascara. Her eyes spoke volumes and I instantly warmed up to her. She smiled. I smiled.

"Do you know what time it is?"

Did I know what time it was? Questions like this were acute reminders that God had a personal vendetta towards me. I should have ignored her.

—No, sorry.

An old man glanced up, mumbled the time, then returned to his paper. From the headlines, I could tell he was reading some article dealing with Iraq. The Middle East was a synonym for crisis. It never ceased to amaze me what people would do for a piece of that desert soil—the Holy Land!

"Thanks," she said, her eyes fixed on mine.

The old man nodded.

Ding-dong. "Stand clear of the closing doors. Forty-Second Street." Before the doors closed she stopped and looked back straight at me–into me–as if she knew. Her eyes glinted in a peculiar way. I saw an unnatural flash of white canines as she smiled, then walked away.

I fought the urge to follow her. *Ding-dong.* Doors closed. She was gone.

The ridiculous moment was over in the blink of an eye. I shook the illusion—the fanged smile, the sarcastic woman–from my memory. The thought of the Others came and went, like the ocean in its unfailing faithfulness to the moon. The knowledge of other cursed souls wandering the Earth filled me with dread, but also with awe–the kind of awe a child might experience when he first realizes that he's not unique. I preferred not to think about these others and avoided them at all costs.

I lived in a constant state of denial, believing that if I abstained from recognizing their presence, they would stop existing altogether. The thought of these predators walking the same streets I did, or watching me from a distance, sent pangs of fear to my core. I was young by their exaggerated standards and worse, I was weak. This terror, unlike all my other discomforts, was very real, as real as Goddamned children feeding on human blood.

I knew of human groups that worshipped Them, paying homage with blood sacrifices and often fatal rituals. I had come upon such a group a few years back while traversing the depths of the park. They had captured a woman and were cutting precise incisions into her body. The blood that poured from these sacramental lacerations was black in the deep purple of that scene.

As I sought to get away, I was held in place by a rippling, bending sound that folded and multiplied until it toppled my knees. It was an ancient call from an unknown place–in our language—if there were such a thing. The sound was primal, forceful like a sledge striking iron. My body fought the pull and lost.

Within moments the blaring vibration became an enchanting melody. It intoxicated me. Beneath the sweet was a bitter offensiveness, a dolorous suffering I found unbearable.

The girl-child bled profusely. I remembered the loss of control, the overwhelming urge to feed. Augmented by the sublime human voices, I crawled towards Them through the woods. I knew there were Others, but I couldn't see them. I was blinded by desire, by the harmonic voices, by the rich, nourishing liquid that lay only paces away. Then, I felt the pain—more tangible than any suffering, colder than the harshest winter.

My body coughed up its blood as agonizing talons pierced deep, scalding my flesh like acid—like sunlight! Whatever held me captive dispersed, leaving me soaked in my own blood. The world became a fiery red haze, then went dark. My ears no longer heard, my eyes no longer saw. Those voices circled my mind like a murder of crows raping my normalcy, bringing with them my own screams, elevating me to an all-new sensation—mortality.

Ding-dong. "West Fourth Street is next. Stand clear of the closing doors, please." I looked past the paradise of darkness beyond the scratched window. Every so often, as the train sped past an illuminated niche, I saw the elaborately scribbled tag names on the walls. For those who lived in these tunnels, the walls were indeed their canvases—their one chance to immortalize their name and therefore their existence. Lovers attempted the same when they scratched their initials into the bark of old trees. They believed that a physical manifestation of their love would indeed make that passing emotion last forever. These brave souls who walked along the narrow passageways with their supply of spray paint were keeping their names alive forever. They wanted all to see that they had braved the train and won.

With the opening of the train's doors I felt exposed, open, as if the wind in the tunnel would splinter me to pieces. My thoughts turned to the escort I had met beneath the rain. Anna, whose voice had soothed, and whose gentle fingers coaxed life out of Scarlatti's clavichord, would cross my path again. The city was too small to keep us apart for long.

Streets wound like serpents heading south. The cold, I believed, was not good for the soul. The cold sought out all crevasses and all sanctuaries. It stiffened the fingers, hardened the heart, and twisted the face in a grimace of violation. Cold people stared out of half-closed lids waiting to exhale, their eyes locked on a final destination. No one looked my way. No one noticed that my breath, unlike theirs, caused no disturbance, no fog, and no warmth. My body exuded no heat, no salty perspiration—no life.

I stood still, leaning against a pole, hands in pockets, feigning cold like the good actor I was. Across the street in the orange glow of pinewood and tropical-painted walls, strangers gathered for coffee and hot chocolate. The music coming from inside was something slow and mellow, the type of music you heard everywhere but never really listened to. Several couples chatted as they sipped from oversized pastel mugs. *Tres chic!* Like conquistadors, these natives had probably come from some remote mid-western town to lay claim to this spot of tropical city. By the door, two women giggled, their hefty backpacks resting against the bookshelves. Tourists. Blonde. Young. Anything could befall two lonely women in a far off country, especially in a city so burdened by crime. Not exactly my style, but... nice legs.

Ignoring at least four beggars, I waited. Finally, the girls made their way out of the coffee shop. They passed right by me as they hurried towards the subway. Their aroma, faint with the promise of supple flesh and hidden pain, complicated my hunger. I struggled to stay focused.

Youth bloomed in these two, like a bittersweet song of all that was brief and already wilting. I had seen plenty of similar complexions—flawless, but altogether helpless against the elements. The cold dried their skin, the heat caused rashes, and soon there would be wrinkles on their mother-of-pearl veneer. They would wither along with their youthful idealism. I would give them a chance to avoid that disillusion. Their perfect faces would be remembered as they were, not as they would be found—later.

Ah, German! Out of their mouths the language seemed much sweeter. German was a forceful tongue, demanding to be spoken with personality, something that these two doe-eyed fauns utterly lacked. I followed the pair like a dog, letting myself be carried by their scent. My heart beat to the hypnotic pulse of their enthusiasm.

Warm air rose out of the tunnel providing a split-second of heat. I inhaled the mustiness, the humidity, and the wetness of the subterranean with its odd mixture of urine and rat droppings. In that thick atmosphere there lingered the sultry smell of flesh and sweat, of nervousness and dreams deferred. The bowels of the city carried the burden of the lofty heights, where people moved within crystal-glass hallways. Midway down, the clouds graced the well-to-do's privileged vision, obscuring the layers of unfortunates who squirmed below. When the rich toasted, with smiles like butter, they condemned all that lay beneath their winged feet. Large rats scurried about, a metaphor for all who dwelled where the sun refused to shine.

At the sight of the rats the two girls squirmed, backing off the yellow strip along the platform. Stupidly, they unfurled the large map of the known underground to begin calculating their return to safety. I leaned against the beam, watching the two girls lazily.

The taller girl was built like a house on stilts with large, sea-green eyes and a round, unmemorable face. The younger one was pouty, shorter, with an air of importance about her that intrigued me. She was also prettier. I spied her nipples peaking against the gray thermal sweater she wore. She would be fun!

I followed my unsuspecting victims, letting my imagination get the best of me. Every footstep sparked a tingle of anticipation. I felt a pull in my loins which demanded satisfaction. I imagined licking their porcelain skin, biting those nipples, and kissing those young, unblemished lips. I would drink from their bodies and have myself an Oktoberfest in December!

Many a time had I fantasized about making love to a woman, but when the hunger called—Devil's marionette that I was—I fed, maimed and killed that which I desired to love. When damnation whispered in my ears, the world warped and receded and became red with promised heat. Blood made me hot and in that molten heat, my fantasies vanished. Illusions of Time and of saturated lust-love dispersed with the frenzied beat behind my temples.

I yearned desperately for the love of a woman—to feel gentle fingers caress, scratch, tease. I longed for supple thighs, hot and quivering, to wrap around my waist. I craved looks of abandon, bodies colliding as one. I was still, in so many ways, a Man, hungering for that singular condition denied to me—Life! I envisioned, momentarily, Anna's honeyed breath upon my neck. How alive I had felt in my poor man's paradise! The passions that had melted our insides, stretched our senses to the limit. When the sun rose, stinging our sleepless eyes, my Anna and I knew we were truly alive.

When youth filled my soul I could wake to a love which I believed would last forever. Youth! Innocent and unsuspecting, passive, dumb, and altogether wonderful! Before me, the two German girls teased me in the way they went about their business. It was as if they knew the inevitable was coming and were delaying it by poking their heads into every souvenir shop along Broadway. Unbelievable!

As I trailed them, Juliet entered my mind. Her youth had been painfully etched in my head. Every time I polished her radiant limbs, I held back the tears—and the guilt. I kissed those red-lined lips and smoothed that raven hair with the palms of my hands, until I was blinded by hunger. She had known all along. I was convinced that she knew when a smile crossed her lips as her eyelids closed with the silence of death. I battled the sun to remain with her. I stayed with her for many nights, crying her blood, knowing that God was laughing somewhere... out there.

Juliet's last moments were spent returning Death's kiss—my kiss! Why she chose to die that way, I shall never know, but no amount of earthly pain was worth the type of suffering I brought to her. Almost sixty years later, I still mourned my gentle Juliet, a being who, like myself, was thrust into the world to suffer.

Having had their fill of plastic key rings and Statue of Liberty magnets, the German girls made their way to their hotel. All around me restless people walked in and out of bars, theaters, stores, and restaurants. They had that stupefied it's-Friday-night look on their faces. A row of people stood with open briefcases around their necks, selling black-market watches that glimmered beneath the entertaining array of Times Square lights. Others had set up shop selling instant cameras, while a group of Asian artists sat on their canvas chairs sketching charcoal portraits. In the corner a group of kids banged out tunes on empty buckets as their comrades break-danced for a dumbfounded crowd. I observed as they twisted and spun their bodies, contorting and popping as if they were made of rubber. They were talented, and I was content to see the German girls avoid the spectacle.

The two girls were like fragile reeds swaying in the breeze. Their dainty movements brought to life those memories of long ago, when I used to sit and stare at the traveling puppeteers and their makeshift marionettes. I recalled the carved wooden limbs as they trembled to life beneath those masterful strings, only to lie limp and lifeless after the crowds departed and the laughter ceased.

Marionettes. Distracting marionettes held aloft by ropes. How I loved to wrench them off the floor, levitating them like butterflies and watching the blood flow. Blood. Oh God, sweet blood, spilling, filled with heat and oblivion. Ecstasy. Mouthfuls of desire. Life.

I... I needed to stop...

A knot of hunger tied itself into the pit of my stomach. It called and called until it became deafening. All other sounds drowned. My head swam in agony. Heartbeats pounded the sides of my temples like a stampeding herd. Monotonous. Thunderous. Iron hammers beating upon red-hot anvils. Then the slow, painful protrusion of fangs. Blinding lights beat down into my ancient brain. The world became blue, like velvet, the only color of love.

Juliet!

I was losing...

The living passed me by. They were everywhere— emerging from the azure haze. All their hearts galloped simultaneously, a blur of sound, like the flapping of wings. Someone was trying to speak to me, but his voice came to my ears distant and slow. I pushed them aside like bowling pins and they wobbled as they fell upon each other. I felt unholy fire in all my extremities. The hunger would not wait. It was endless.

I stumbled, half mad, into an entrance-way. I scampered away from the heartbeats up the winding stairs with useless palms pressed to my ears. I still heard their voices in the distance, somewhere. I climbed higher and higher. The sound came again. I moved with the involuntary secrecy of a predator. The call inside me was steady, like a metronome. A symphony could have been played upon the voice's rhythm. My eyes adjusted to the darkness. When the blue fog lifted from my senses, I stood poised, my entire being focused on the sound. That eternal beating of life, divinity itself made manifest, assaulted my deadened cells. Getting closer.

I turned the corner, hungry, expectant.

Nothing.

I climbed higher, to the next flight.

Nothing!

I kicked the rusty door of the roof wide open and stepped into the cold night. With each turn of my head, the city stretched into a dizzying array of light. Trails of motion converged before my eyes. The perfect heartbeat continued to crash my perception until I lost my balance. I fell to my hands and knees upon the tar rooftop. I crawled towards the shadows. The sound of blood whispered like a lover.

Then the glorious voice broke the spell.

"So, you are he whom the others talk about? What a pleasant surprise to see you. And in such a vulnerable position—crawling on all fours!"

The laughter echoed in my head. Her voice was perfect, flawless in timbre and pitch. I hung suspended in its power, trying to memorize each note.

For a moment I thought the voice Anna's, but it was a foolish hope. It wasn't even a voice, it was a feeling. It was all feelings distilled. For a moment I felt free, as if released from the bondage of all other voices. I wondered if mortals experienced this sensation when I spoke to them. The voice in my blood called out and I answered. I obeyed hoping that it would be the end of me. I knew that I could not refuse it anything.

This being who addressed me was ancient. I had heard it before. In the past? When? When in the past? Where had I heard this calling before?

Heart beating, yet not human. Something else. The hairs on my neck stood up, and I felt that sensation of wanting to sprint, to run away. Whatever was in the shadows was from another place–another time. It was something utterly incomprehensible to me. It was unlike me, and I trembled. I looked up one last time, peering deep into the shadows and beyond. I was being torn apart from the inside out. I fought. The melodious voice came again, then faded along with the rest of the world.

It was summer. The cool breeze that rose off the river carried with it the scent of restlessness. The woman exhaled, tried to move. The fan above us hummed as it turned, circulating the humid hot air about the room. The white sheets, now red, were damp with sweat and blood. Through the windows above French doors the night crept in, silent and starless like a black, endless ocean. The sounds of a badly tuned piano trailed in.

My caramel goddess awakened while the sun was still high, but she was too weak to move. Her raven-black curls clung to her wet skin. Her coffee-brown eyes spoke what her parched lips could not. Her breathing came in short gasps. Her heart labored to stay alive.

Her eyes traveled to a painting of banana trees on the far wall and lingered there for a moment before they closed once again. Her fingers clutched the sheets as she made an effort to pull herself forward. Her muscles tensed from the strain. A new layer of sweat broke out upon her forehead.

The scent of magnolias made my goddess happy when she was a young girl. She confessed her first love was among the boys that came around selling ice cream and lemonade. Lemonade, how she loved refreshing lemonade with star-shaped ice cubes like her grandmother used to make. She cried.

The howls of bloodthirsty men filled me with dread as my legs pushed forward. Their torches shone through the trees, beacons piercing the heavy fog. The men closed in on me like vengeful beasts, holding weapons in their hands. Out of their mouths came a stream of curses as they crossed themselves and set their dogs upon me. The growling became louder, the lights brighter. The mob was all around me, surrounding me. Angry faces peered through the silhouette of trees. The ground swallowed my every step, slowing my escape. I sank in that mud and tripped again and again, until I thought I could not go on.

A dog leaped up in the darkness. I saw a flash of its reflective eyes as its teeth locked around my throat. Pain crackled through my limbs, blood spurted from my throat, then trickled down to the earth to be swallowed. Life trickled out of me. The blood! My life! I clawed at the beast with the remainder of my strength. Somehow, I tore the dog from my throat, snapped its neck. I sank down into the mud with it cradled in my arms. I ravenously bit deep into its matted fur in search of blood.

At first the nourishing liquid filled me with strength, then the excruciating burn engulfed me from the inside out. I stumbled, poisoned, into the fog. The voices were getting closer. My eyes closed.

I felt their stabs and slashes from all sides. They had caught up to me. With picks and shovels they beat me beyond pain, beyond unconsciousness, beyond recognition. All the blood in my immortal body seeped out from the lacerations and cut-off limbs.

I was very deep. I felt the earth caving in—oppressing me. My body felt drained of life, my eyes ached, my limbs were trapped. I cursed God. The chill that made my bones its home was colder than ice. The earth accepted me, healed me, only to torture me another day.

Where had all the time gone? Where were the sugary, candlelit moments when I was still able to taste and enjoy the flesh for its own sake? Only fragmented memories remained of times past when luscious lips whispered sweet nothings in my ear. Where were the arms and thighs that held me close in steamy red interiors? Where were the coy girls who swarmed around me like moths, feeding me juicy bits of fruit? When did I retreat into the depths of the underground? When did immortality take its toll upon my soul? When did the blood become so irresistible as to stand in the way of my humanity?

I believed, and still do, that there is nothing more inspiring than the sight of a beautiful woman. I still remembered the endless nights spent at that house of ill repute in the Latin Quarter, where every whore was a queen. They stood akimbo at the foot of the stairs, eyeing me like a piece of meat. They were tainted, living on the fringe of society, catering to everyone and anyone.

The harlots' robes fascinated me; some were silk, others velvet or satin, embroidered in golden and silver threads. Sometimes I imagined that I was in a cage filled with rare and exotic birds, each brighter than the next. The patterns on the robes formed a rebus of color that confounded the senses. The robes concealed and revealed simultaneously, casting an exquisite spell of seduction. Underneath the luscious fabrics I caught glimpses of stockings and frilly garments to be undone.

Occasionally, I caught glimpses of navels and thighs or hard, brown nipples. These girls, with eyes wide, often innocent-looking, were vicious creatures of pleasure. Their bodies radiated an infernal lasciviousness that was both inviting and nauseating and on some nights I disbelieved that they were girls at all.

I had regained consciousness some time ago, perhaps hours or days or even weeks ago. I could not remember. Some of the dreams and scattered thoughts remained fresh, but all else vanished from my mind. My mother was still in my head, keeping alive my hope for repentance. Anna was there also, swimming in the pool of my disjointed thoughts. Somewhere along a hidden stretch of beach Anna was waiting for me. Waiting also were my sick little habits. The caged-up souls beneath the floorboards were still alive.

What if this was it, what if it was the end of the line? I wondered. Was death nothing but a tomb of thoughts? The irony made me smile. It made sense. God's plans always made sense in some fucked-up way.

The world was pathetic. It was random and chaotic and filled with misery—a chunk of spinning rock in a random fucking void. I lived on a rock that miraculously sprouted life: First bacteria, then monstrous animals and finally man—no better than bacteria, and more monstrous than the dinosaurs. Cynical, wicked, and unpredictable, that was Man, truly the most imperfect and ridiculous creation to ever cross God's mind.

I rotted beneath the earth. I returned to life. I rotted again. The idea was comical, existentialist actually. I was beginning to believe there was nothing beyond my vicious cycle. Was this the end?

Where was the tunnel and the light? Where were the souls to greet me on the other side? Where was my welcoming party? Where were all those people whose life I had either ended or ruined? WHERE?

I imagined the earth turning on its axis, the noonday clouds whirling above me, the warmth of a summer's breeze. In the distance, a young woman calling out to her lover through the sugar cane fields. I heard the neighing of horses, the buzzing of bees and the movement of the blades of grass.

As my vision sunk below the surface, I smelled the topsoil where ants, beetles, crickets and insects made their home. I became acutely aware of each grain of soil, each stone, each rivulet of moisture as it fed the roots of trees. Deeper still, as the chill of unfathomable depths extinguished all life, I heard my inner screams echoed. I needed blood or I would never rise again.

My head ached. I was not so much a prisoner of my subterranean grave as a captive of my thoughts. Who was that on the roof? What had happened back there? Was I even in the city? Was it all a dream? I needed this like a hole in my head. Jesus fucking Christ! I needed to get out of here!

The waves came and went. I allowed their soothing softness to wash over me. In the distance, the horizon curved on either side, proving that the earth was, indeed, spherical. That was the news of the day.

AN ENDLESS HUNGER

Cristobal had shocked many with his decision to sail to India. The sun was high in the sky, and a delicious heat permeated my body. Crystalline waters left their foamy imprints along white beaches. Prior to our arrival, the New World thrived in balanced order. Now, red-lipped whores sauntered the streets with drunken men. Black skin mixed with white. I closed my eyes to that blinding light and stretched upon the shore.

The colors of the tropics were brighter, more opulent in their splendor than all the Royal Courts of Europe. The reds vibrated with life, while the blues, rich as tourmaline, absorbed all woes. In the salty air, the perfume of mango mingled with the delicate aroma of hibiscus.

All my life I had been running, fearing, denying who I was, waiting for fate to hand me courage on a silver platter. Guilt-ridden, I whipped myself to repent my mother's death. I roamed the streets as a scavenger. I became the jackal of dark and dingy alleyways, hiding in the shadows, ready to strike back at a society that owed me something. I was young. I was stupid. Worst of all, I was spineless.

Thoughts came and went in those insufferable hours, days, weeks. I had no sense of time. I existed above time, above all the things that made one human. Whatever had done this to me would pay. I would not rest until I found it again, the voice—it was so beautiful. Its sound had brought tears to my eyes. I wanted to be back on that rooftop clinging to that glorious heartbeat.

I was alive again by the shore, crying, kissing the sunlit sand! The ocean sparkled in the distance like fine glass as the sound of warm waves made me aware of my own heart beating inside my body. My lungs inhaled that opiate air with a vengeance. I took it all in. I fixed my gaze where sea met sky. Then I stared at the sun.

I heard things stirring in the earth and it terrified me. My body became excruciatingly frigid as I returned to life–death. I awoke, screaming...

A month passed before I rose from my earthen prison.

My body dematerialized against my will. Like a wisp of smoke I rose through the earth. I stood in the familiar surroundings of my decaying hole. I had lain conscious beneath the earth for countless days and nights harvesting my splintered memories.

Blood sweat broke upon my brow. My knees felt weak and brittle. I collapsed to the floor and rolled myself up into a ball. The heartbeat returned, pounding my ears as the voice raped my defenses. I rocked back and forth.

Juliet stood in the doorway. Arms crossed, hair pulled neatly back, Juliet's fiery lips moved. I didn't hear her words until much later.

—Pull yourself together. Go downstairs.

I was afraid, paranoid that I was being watched. That thing in my dream had not been human, and I could yet recall with crystal clarity the sound of that beautiful heartbeat.

When I opened my eyes and looked towards the door, she was gone. Emptiness greeted me. The vertigo of my nightmare faded and the room came into focus again. I turned over on my side and crawled to the gushing pipe. Cold water splashed into the basin and I vehemently scrubbed every inch of my body. I felt dizzy and disoriented—a dull pain stretching and growing behind my eyes. I wanted to cry. I needed blood.

As I settled into the ordinariness of my surroundings my nostrils picked up the scent of death and dust and suffering. I heard in my head all their voices, the lamentations, the laughter, and it was joyous. I had never been so happy and so tormented in my long unlife. My captives, if not dead, were no doubt thinner.

I walked cautiously down the stairs to my clavichord. As in my dream, Anna's scarf lingered there–untouched. The knit scarf–an item already part of my memories–was covered by a film of dust. I held it to my cheek and inhaled its luscious perfume of jasmine and moisture. In the corner, by the golden mirror, Anna lay slumped against the wall. She was pale, sickly and very small. Her chest heaved with great effort beneath her coat. Her heart yet fought for life. Anna would not live long without medical attention.

She was barely eighteen. Her thoughts yielded a half-sister, some cousins she hadn't seen in years, an abusive father, and an overall fucked-up life. She worked in a greasy diner during the day. Hated it. Anna was loveless, passionless, and artless. Her mother had wanted her to become a concert pianist, but those dreams were deferred by her mother's death. Inside Anna reigned pain and disillusionment, fear and aggression. She had grown up across the river, west of the city in a roach-infested apartment on Golden Lane. The irony was profound.

Anna sensed the intrusion, felt my presence, and shuddered. I smelled her. I knew what she would taste like. I saw right through her. I witnessed her countless nights with half-drunk strangers, the foreign lips and fake words, the anxiety as she undressed time and time again in dimly lit hotel rooms or in the backseat of limos. I saw her gazing into the mirrors of restaurant bathrooms, reapplying her lipstick, her face blank of emotion. Unlike my Anna from so long ago, this Anna was tired of serving tables and men. Her soul was an open, wordless book. She had everything and nothing. She was young and old, black and white. She was like me.

—Anna? Come out of there, my dear.

Gazing deeper, probing further, I saw crumpled music sheets and cheap perfume, an abusive boyfriend much older than her. Fistfights and sleepless nights. Vegas. Bright lights. Lonely drives through the desert near dawn. A girl with an overactive imagination. Thoughts of a charming prince in shining armor, of breakfast in bed, of school, and a normal life. She was fourteen. A runaway. Her mother was dead and buried in a small-town cemetery. Her piano was abandoned in the messy living room of their one-bedroom apartment.

I saw in the darkness as rough hands caressed Anna's smooth shoulders and legs. I tasted her bitter tears as she looked out the window that faced the alley. The skeletal framework of black fire-escapes hung over the street like spider webs. I understood why Anna ran, why she fled that dreadful place. I understood her temper during mornings when her father asked her to cook breakfast. I could feel his lascivious stare on her nubile body, could sense his lust through her fear and loathing of him. I tasted her father's tongue as it forced its way into her mouth, smelled the liquor on his breath, the roughness of his beard. I burned with rage as his callused hands wormed beneath her skirt.

I felt Anna's struggle, her confusion as her fists pounded uselessly against her father's body. I heard her screaming, pleading, crying as he forced himself into her time and time again. She tried to scratch, to kick and bite, but she was powerless against him. Then came the pain as her father struck her beautifully disheveled young face. Blackness. Soft apologies. Distant sobbing. I had seen too much.

I had seen a long-buried part of myself.

Anna shuddered, sinking deeper into the shadows. Her eyes fluttered open and I was startled at the dark fire in them. She was pale, her lips and cheeks had lost their rosy hue, but her beauty remained fresh–disarming.

I was drawn to her, entranced by her empty dignity. She was so much like me. She was so alone.

To my surprise, Anna grabbed hold of the mirror's frame and pulled herself up. She stood before me like the statue of the Virgin herself—like those exquisite Catholic icons, forever frozen in the adoration of the Christ. I wanted to reach out to her, to hold her and comb her tangled hair, to soothe the hunger that ate her insides, to quench the thirst that plagued her slender throat. I wanted to be her air, her sun, her love, but it was not to be.

The hunger called, yet I didn't move. She looked into me, beyond me, and understood her purpose as the lamb understands his in the presence of the lion. I heard my voice echo in the cavernous chamber. I sounded distant and strange when I said her name.

—Anna.

Her silence both intrigued and excited me. Absent were the streams of curses and complaints and the many creative ways in which my victims begged for their pathetic lives. She was stoic, and in her self-possessed stance, she was willing to die—facing the end without ever giving me the luxury of self-pity. Our eyes locked and dueled for an eternity before I finally looked away, feeling self-conscious.

I ran cold fingers through my hair, then looked down at the floor. Beneath, I heard the squirming of sweaty people slowly starving to death. The silence was unbearable between Anna and I. I wanted to kiss her and make love to her. It was perverse. Inside me the hunger stirred and called, unreasonable and capricious. Her unwavering stare made me feel insecure. I didn't understand what was happening to me.

She took a step towards me, her large eyes capturing my every move. My desire for the fragile girl grew and grew until I thought I would rip her apart if she dared move closer. I stood unmoving, unable to act or react or do anything at all. I could only watch as each step brought her closer to me.

I felt out of control, blind, and hungry. The room faded to a dull gray, and all the color was lost save for the green of her glorious eyes, the silky blackness of her hair, and the bloody-red, unbuttoned coat. I feasted on her, my eyes darting from her eyes to her lips down to the fine curve of her sculpted throat and then lower still to the curve of her breasts and waist and hips. She was barefoot. Each of her steps left a footprint on the dust. Anna was like an angel sent from heaven to torture me.

Anna's hands reached around her shoulders as she let slip the heavy coat. Beneath, she wore a sleeveless dress the color of sapphires that came down an inch below her perfect knees. On her left hand she wore a marquisette ring that sparkled in the half-light like diamonds.

She approached me as quietly as a cat. Slowly, the distance between us diminished until we were but an arm's length from each other. Anna made my entire body tremble.

I thought I might break if she touched me.

In her eyes I saw my own discomfort as I backed up into a large table, knocking a vase of desiccated flowers to the ground. The urn shattered, breaking the silence. The dried reeds and roses spilled amidst the bone-white shards of ceramic. Anna continued to look straight into my eyes, but something had changed. She ceased her advance. Her stare grew softer.

I was distinctly aware of the attraction between us. Between our very different fears was a raw and uncontrollable desire to be loved. I needed this child-woman, like blood, like night, like my Mother and Anna, and at one point God and his pantheon of satirical saints. I needed her as I had needed my Golden Woman, my saviors—my victims.

The idea that I should love this pathetic girl, this abused and beautiful whore was utterly ridiculous, but for the moment, true. Yes! True! Anna, my beautiful whore, was reincarnated in the form of some strange, starving girl. It felt like madness.

I closed my mind to hers.

I didn't want to know what she thought of me, of my wretched existence, of what I did every night, of how I killed, and lived and died. I didn't want Anna to know. I didn't want to kill her, but the hunger needed no consent.

When Juliet had left this world forever, it horrified me. Her pearly skin turned cold to the touch, and her eyes glossed over, fixing me with an accusatory stare. I remembered the desire to turn and run and never stop, but instead, I immortalized her in bronze.

I didn't want the same for Anna. I didn't want her lifeless eyes, her warm flesh buried in cold metal. I wanted her as she was before me now—alive! I wanted to yell at her, to tell her to flee, get away, but instead I stood still. Leaning against the table, frightened at the thought of her death, I cringed as she took another step forward.

Anna came closer and closer until I could feel her hot breath against my chest. Shockingly, she pressed her soft body against mine, wrapping her arms around my back. I gasped. She leaned her cheek against my chest and a solitary tear rolled down onto the white cotton of my shirt. Heat rose from her body like perfume.

I began to tremble as she held me in the darkness, and before I could stop myself, my arms reciprocated her embrace. I pulled her tightly against me, using every ounce of willpower to stave off the hunger. The closeness between us felt pure. I felt needed and loved. The voices stilled. I looked up beyond the ceiling, beyond the fountain of my angel, beyond the sky and clouds. I looked for heaven, but I was already there.

When we obeyed the pull between our bodies, our mouths clashed. The kiss melted my insides. An intoxicating wave of warmth rushed through me. As her lips parted I sought her tongue. I drowned in the ecstasy of our contact.

I heard the blood rush through her veins, through the aorta and the capillaries beneath her skin. I felt her body blush beneath the blue dress. She was hot and wet and full of life and blood. I wanted her, I wanted to kiss and lick her all over. I wanted to bury myself inside her—to eat her alive!

My mind swam in the languorous sweetness of Anna's kiss. I bit down. The taste of her was euphoric. I closed my eyes and savored her blood. I suckled the tiny wound on her lip like a child might a mother's teat. I was delightedly happy and warm. I dragged Anna to the floor. I crawled on top of her–my body burning.

Dim recollections of supple breasts and hot thighs, of long, girlish arms, and of lips wet with anticipation flooded my mind. My hands remembered her softness, the swell of her curves, her pleasured eyes as the dress slid past her hips, all the way down. Anna lay beneath me like a bare-breasted goddess. I answered her invitations, bit deep into her maelstrom of dreams to savor every fear imaginable.

Such deep sorrow it was to have loved and lost, to have given every last breath to an ideal and lost. Sadness. The silence between Anna and I widened and grew into an impassable chasm. I felt her defeat. Anna's body and soul gradually withered before me. Terrified, I coiled into myself, into the refuge of tears and cowardliness that I had built for myself. I felt sick at the thought of having hurt her, sick at having to look at her dying body upon my floor. Barely alive, Anna's heart tormented me with its labored plea. I cried. I screamed my sorrows into the emptiness.

–Why, God? WHY?!

I wanted to breathe life back into her. I wanted to tear myself into pieces.

Anna's dying thoughts told a tale of a pale and cloudless sky, cool with the colors of impending night. Shadows stretched wraith-like on the desert floor, scurrying from the sun into unknown wilds. Her loneliness was broken only by the distant howls of coyotes in search of food. The comfort of her visions was innocently beautiful–pure like a fresh snowfall. Rage was absent from her final thoughts. Anna's skies, like my skies long ago, were bright and blue and through her mind's eye, I saw the sun set.

———————————————————

Anna's blood had made me warm. In that heat, the dilapidated curtains returned to their youthful splendor. Golden women gossiped and gleamed from atop their pedestals. In the roughness of the stone above my head I thought I saw yellow butterflies. Anna's hand lay on top of mine like a feather weight. My fingers closed around hers.

—Look up, Anna. Look! Blue skies and butterflies, just like in your dreams.

The scream in my head could only be compared to the cries of hundreds of hungry infants. My mind was about to burst. What I had done to her was maddening. Shreds of clothing lay scattered about—torn from her body. Her hair was soaked and matted with her own blood, which congealed around her in a crimson outline. Darkness in the shade of bruises covered her arms where my fingers had held her lovingly close. Above her left breast was a gash, still bleeding, from where I had taken my fill. Her closed eyelids and lips were a deep plum color, eerie in their stillness. I tried to rise from my blood-gorged stupor to clot the few drops of blood still left in her.

I had no memories of how I had hurt her. Nothing in my mind could justify the way she looked. How had our sweet embrace turned so brutal? Had I really done this to her? My nervous fingers held rags to her many bite wounds where blood continued to flow. Visions of my pious mother sweating, shivering, and disfigured by the pestilence resurfaced, filling me with anguish and hopelessness.

Juliet looked on quietly as I tore the blue velvet curtains from the ceiling hooks. The fabric fell heavily to the floor, sending a cloud of dust into the air. Bereft of the curtains, the statue of Juliet looked lopsided and cheap, no longer as magnificent as I remembered. The air was musty, old, a reflection of my soul. I was saturated by the emptiness, hypnotized by my descent into despair. I felt powerless. I was.

What could I do if Anna stopped fighting, if she gave in to death? What could I do if her lungs refused another breath, if her tired mind gave up her body? If her soul forsook this world for another?

My mind raced through the possibilities. I focused on her fading vision of the desert as the sky continued to change from cobalt to rust and finally darkened to indigo. The prisoners under the floorboards were silent, or perhaps I had ousted them from my mind, cursing them to whatever destiny hunger inspired.

Anna's heart still beat in my ears. I held the heavy cloth of the curtains now, indecisive, feeling as though my actions were futile. I was farming in the sea, as an old friend once told me. Although I had no reason, I had every reason to help her. I would not let her fall, not like the others, not like the cold, golden women, not like my Mother or Anna of long ago.

This girl would live, because I willed it. Anna the call girl would live. She would live and be free from me–free to forget my face forever. I burned inside. I felt dizzy with pressure. I liked it. I watched as the treacherous heat escaped her body. I remembered her fingers gliding on the keys of the old clavichord, as the hammers hit the taut strings, producing that flight of thunderous notes that filled the staleness and drove back bleakness. I remembered seeing Anna for the first time through the wet panes of the cab's windows. I remembered calling her agency and requesting her company under a false name.

I remembered loving her, desiring her, touching her beautiful skin, kissing her supple lips, until both our worlds faded into a red bliss—a symphony of hunger as I consumed her life.

I couldn't wait any longer.

Time was always against me.

Death was quicker than life–a blink of an eye.

A breath.

Death was the quickest of God's messengers.

I wrapped my cold and shivering Anna with the dense cloth. Heat began to return to her body. I held her close, all the time fighting the tears that threatened, with each step, to choke me. I fled upwards and outwards with the girl in my arms. The heavy stone, guardian of my nothings, moved with ease. The familiar gloom of the hollows beneath the park spiraled past me at great speed.

As my legs pushed us through the depths of the tunnels, I caught glimpses of faces, fires, and pockets where the once-socialized denizens of society huddled for warmth. The city above my head had no scruples. It had forgotten these lost people.

My heart was etched with anguish. My thoughts pushed me precariously forward, into Anna's own mind, until the arid air of the desert returned to my nostrils with full force. Ahead, my eyes saw everything and nothing. I was one with her as we stumbled into the familiar circle where the angel waited.

The ground beneath my feet was still spinning from the rush. In Anna's mind the stars shone, silhouetting the walls of the canyons. What was it about that desolate landscape that comforted her? Birds circled and disappeared behind the massive formations of rock, then swooped down and pecked at her dead eyes. I turned, looked around, dismissing the panic of my thoughts.

Beyond the desiccated limbs of the winter trees the moon sat in full-orbed splendor. I ran like a madman past the lit promenade of golden arches where the stairs rose elegantly to the top of the terrace. I was desperate.

The darkness told the story of the city. The air carried with it the scent of sex and violence, of murder and rape and a dozen other unaccounted-for crimes.

My mother lay in a corner, sweating, the sores on her skin turning a deep red, then bursting with pus. The fever consumed her day and night, until her cheeks were those of a corpse and her eyes stared straight ahead into the emptiness, barely blinking. She had lost the ability to speak. She was sunken, shriveled, frightening to look upon. Her lips were drawn, her face frozen in an endless scream.

Anna was still breathing when the cab pulled over. I shoved her wrapped, feeble form into the backseat.

"Hey man, what do you think you are doing?"

—I need you to take her to a hospital.

"No! I don't want no junkie in my backseat! Get her out of my car!"

—Take her to the nearest hospital. Now!

I took some crumpled money out of my pockets and threw it at the driver. The act made me uneasy.

"Fuck, man!"

No scruples, no regrets. I slammed the door and ran back into the park, disappearing before the driver had a chance to get out. Through the trees I watched the cabbie. He took one look at Anna's pale face and stepped on the gas. I heard him call 911 as he drove away.

—Goodbye, Anna.

ABOUT NARCISSE NAVARRE

Narcisse Navarre was born in Habana, Cuba in 1975. She grew up surrounded by nature in a world nearly devoid of media. Prompted by her father's nightly tales of the Greek Gods, folklore and magic, Narcisse's imagination blossomed into an extraordinary force in her life.

In 1984 she emigrated to the United States where she was able to realize her dream of becoming an artist, poet and author. Spiritual, fiery and passionate, Narcisse is an avid world traveler and adventure seeker. Whether she is wreck diving, zipping through Belizian jungles or strolling through Roman ruins, Narcisse is always looking for way to incorporate her experiences into her writing.

Currently, Narcisse is co-authoring a trilogy of dark fantasy novels.

For more information visit:
Khajj.com, NarcisseNavarre.com, DigitalAlchemist.com